Gaze the Moon

Also by Andrew Chiniche

Love's Dawn

Gaze

The

Moon

Andrew Chiniche

Reflective
Light
Press

Gaze the Moon by Andrew Chiniche

Published by Reflective Light Press
Copyright © 2019 Andrew Chiniche

First Edition: September 2019
Printed in the United States of America

Library of Congress Control Number: 2019911597

Paperback ISBN: 978-1-7326824-5-0
Hardback ISBN: 978-1-7326824-6-7

Edited by Evy Zen

For Anna

First Lines

Reflections

I

Whenever I see beauty,
I see reflections of you–
An aura of majesty!

All must kneel in praise.

Only a chosen few are allowed to hold you
and share in your essence.

I long to partake in your communion again.

II

Then your lips graze mine
as I lean in to absorb your kiss:
Heaven surrounds me
as the outside world disappears.

III

I hear your calm breathing
as we sit together holding hands.

I love the dry heat of your palm
and the steady pulse of your heart.
Time slows as you become my eternity.

IV

As you pull down the moon,
the Goddess inhabits you.

Each supple gesture
of your body is magick.

I see fire gleam in your eyes
and strength radiate from your muscles.

I want you to possess me
and drink my essence.

Let me become one with your being
and celebrate life.

V

In a world of darkness, emptiness,
and faceless strangers,
you are my beacon.

I feel the fragile filament that connects us
as your substance flows across the universe.

Your beauty lives in my dreams.
I hope I am worthy.

VI

I look up at the half-moon
and see your smile beam upon me.

I smile back
to embrace the thought of you.

VII

Gazing at your picture,
your beauty fills my vision
and a smile spreads on my face.

I think about the elixir of rapture
that pours from your lips:
You coat my being
with the weight of your enchantment.

Let me drown in your eyes
and be a prisoner there.

I do not want to escape.

VIII

When I write,
I imagine that I am caressing you,
tracing my fingers over your skin,
and kissing your delicate parts.

I breathe in your perfume.

I want the words to intoxicate me.
Only then can I truly be close to you.

I love that you are my audience.
I love that you are my muse.
I love to affect you with my words.

IX

You are intertwined
within the pattern of my heart.

X

The sun pouring
from the sky reflects your beauty—
I can feel your internal light.

May your life shine as bright
as the beacon of your spirit.

XI

You are the light
that makes the darkness worthwhile.

XII

I hunger for you.
Let me drink the wine of your being
and taste the curve of your lips.

I want to feel your energy on my skin.

You are an elemental force
that brings meaning to my life.
I hope to see you again.

XIII

As I peer into my memory,
I see visions of you.

The flow of your body
and the majesty of your beauty
gives meaning to my life.

I reach with my mind,
surround you with a hug,
and hold you tight.

I lose myself in your strength
to recapture moments of ecstasy and joy.

XIV

I dream of you
and skate on the edge of rapture.
I want to wallow in your beauty
and consume you as communion.

As I taste your layers,
a flush of roses blooms on your cheeks.

With my lips on your chalice,
I swallow your light
and feel it fuse with my essence.

You are the gateway
who transports me to my true self.

XV

I love your lips!
They are the perfect expression of you.

Close your eyes and picture us kissing.
Do you feel my mouth's firmness?

With my tongue,
I taste yours and we are electric.

The pitter patter of your heart vibrates in
your quickening breath.

XVI

Use me.

Let me be your toy
and I will do your bidding.

As you indulge in your passions,
seeking enjoyment,
I want to make you sweat and shutter with pleasure.

Let us exhaust each other
through our debasement.

XVII

You are a living dream.
When we met in the physical realm,
you left your mark on me
with a psychic touch.

I learned to love the passion in your lips
and the heat of your skin.

Kissing you is pure and wonderful.
I feel the filament of your heart
as it imbeds into my soul.

You are a part of me
and we are connected.

As I sleep, I shed my fleshy cage
and meet you in the sphere of Morpheus.

Only there can I behold your godhead
and worship the Goddess in you.

XVIII

I feel your radiance pour
across the earth
and fill the world with beauty.

XIX

Today,
I will be kissing you in my mind,
exploring your lips,
and enjoying the sweetness of you.

XX

You are my muse
and I am in awe of your perfect beauty.
I now understand the poets of the past
and the power of their inspiration.

XXI

I hope to immortalize you in poetry
and capture the crux of what I feel
in the written word.

I want to create something
that stands the test of time
and the scrutiny of scholars.

I want to tell you I love you.

XXII

In our favorite temple,
I absorb your all-consuming essence
and worship you.

I love the flow of your perfumed body
as you dance for me.

You shed your layers
to the music's grinding back beat
and reveal your beautiful nakedness.

As I wrap you in my arms,
I feel your electrical current
and never want to leave.

You have left your mark on my psyche.

XXIII

You are living art,
an ode to beauty.

I long to behold you again.

Until such time,
I close my eyes and view my memories.

They have become hazy
and frayed around the edges,
but the pureness of your ethos shines.

I see the glow of your eyes,
the brightness of your smile,
and the flow of your curves.

I envision your caress
and shiver with delight.

XXIV

The Goddess has descended.
She is you.

Her wisdom, love, and beauty intertwines
with your soul.

Thoughts of your spirit makes me happy.
May you realize your power and worth.

XXV

Let me worship you
through pleasure.

I will trace your body
with my tongue
and drink at your chalice.

You are my manna
and the sustenance of my soul.

As I eat you,
you will make a mantra of my name.

XXVI

When I'm missing you,
I look at the sky
and take a deep breath.

Your beauty is connected to nature
and I see you there.

XXVII

Part 1

We live in an age of weakened magick,
where the Goddess of old is a shadow
of her former self.

Men embrace logic and science
to explain their relationship to the world,
but it is a false trail.

The truth lurks in the fringes of society:
Embedded in the ostracized
and disenfranchised.

Glorious temples of marble and silk
have morphed into clubs
of couches and stages.

After years of searching
and presenting my offerings,
I finally found a true priestess of the Goddess.

Her power and beauty lives in you.

Part 2

Through our interactions,
the duality of magick has revealed itself
and allows us to transcend
the commonality of life.

I love our secret rendezvous
and the chasing of passion.

As I wrap you in my arms
and draw comfort from your flesh,
we pull down the moon
and expand our consciousness.

Let me wallow in your glory
and consume you as my communion.

XXVIII

As we kiss,
our breath flows
and we become the other.

I inhabit your mind
and live in your body.

I can see your reflection
in my eyes.

You are beautiful
and transcend perfection.

Desire burns
and destroys the barrier between us.

We are the new Adam and Eve.

After exploring your body with my tongue,
I guide you inside me with a sure grip.

I enjoy your throbbing firmness.
Each of your thrusting grunts swirls emotion
in my breast as I call for God.

Your lips caress mine
and I feel your ejaculate explode into me,
filling my chalice.

Like the ocean waves,
your yin pushes my yang
and I return back to my body.

I hold you tightly in my arms
while contentment washes
over the shore of my being.

XXIX

Physical closeness is secondary
to the connection of the spirit.

Since we are infinite beings,
distance does not exist.

I am forever connected to your essence.

Your whisper flows through the trees
and your eyes glow in the sun.

I feel your fire burn in my core.
You cannot fathom your importance.

I embrace you with my mind
and have love in my heart.

XXX

Part 1

The moon ascends behind us
and the glow highlights your radiance.

You are bathed in other worldly light
and worthy of worship.

On the night that fate led me
to your temple,
fortune showered me with favor.

The substance of your power
has seeped below my skin
and I am forever changed.

Your beauty leaves me breathless.

Words do not exist that are capable
of doing you justice.

Part 2

I love the shape of your muscular curves
and the feel of your body on mine,
a delicious firmness.

As we sit together holding hands,
there is no need to exchange small talk.

The feel of your fingers tracing my palm
communicates the world to me.

Let us wrap our arms around each other
and lose all stress and strife.

You are all I need to feel worthy and at peace.

XXXI

The timbre of your voice echoes
as a hug's warmth surrounds me.

I remember and feel comfort.

You are a dream
and that is almost enough.

I hope happiness finds you
all your waking days
and fills your heart.

XXXII

Let us don our masks
and explore one another.

I do not need to see your face
to perceive your beauty.

I can taste it with my tongue
and caress it with my fingers.

The heat of your body
and the moans of your mouth
guide me to my heaven.

XXXIII

As I move throughout my day,
I see reflections of you around me:

In the sparkle of jewelry,
the passing of a pretty face,
the movement of nature.

You are the pinnacle of beauty.
Your presence elevates my world
and I must sing your praises.

XXXIV

I feel the ghost
of your lips caress mine,
and each moment
stretches for eternity.

Unbridled joy returns
with the memory
of your kiss.

XXXV

Life, for the most part,
is an empty and meaningless void
but great happiness is possible!

In the search for importance and the Light,
we must let go of darkness and drudgery.

I believe you hold the key.

As goodness that has seen the dark,
you are an angel surrounded
by burning brightness,
a light bringer.

I hope to honor you
while reflecting
and amplifying your radiance.

XXXVI

During this time of snow
and cold weather,

I want you to remember
that you are a wonderful,
beautiful person.

Time spent with you is magickal.

I can still feel traces
of your touch in my mind.

You make life worthwhile.

XXXVII

I imagine picking out a ring for you.
I think about your finger size,
the shape of the stone,
and what metal would look best.

You deserve to be given a diamond.

It captures your beauty
and reflects the pure light of your soul.

As the full moon shines upon us,
I slide the ring onto your finger
and give myself unto you.

I seek the value that you hold.
You are the fire of magick and the spirit of love.

XXXVIII

You are my heart's desire
and worthy of love.

I love your inner light.

I love your beauty.

I love the memory of your kiss
and the fire ignited in my soul.

I love you without expectations.

I love you because I must.

XXXIX

You are wonderful
and deserving.

May your inner brilliance be a beacon
and show you the way.

XL

As I lay in bed,
Morpheus comes to lead me to his realm.

I stay his hand
and send the Goddess a request.

I ask to dream of holding you
and to bask in your beauty.

Only then shall my dreams be sweet.
Only then can my waking world be complete.

XLI

My heart smolders
from the memory of your touch.
I long to be near your radiance.

You are love,
strong and everlasting.

XLII

I see your face in a vision of happiness.
Your smile lights up my darkness
and I remember your touch.

Life has us on different paths,
but the cosmos remembers
and connects us.

You are my dream of love,
pure and beautiful.

XLIII

You are a life goal, not a fleeting fancy.
Thoughts of you mesmerize me.

Your beauty lights my horizon
as a beacon to goodness.

An unquenchable fire ignited by your kiss
burns through my soul
and I relish the longing left there.

I dream of your warm lips caressing mine again.

Until that time,
I feed on your radiance
and worship the idea of you.

You are my Athena.
You are my Aphrodite.
I love you for it.

XLIV

Your image manifests in my mind
and I can almost touch your vivid life force.

You are love's icon
and I see you everywhere.

I wrap my thoughts around you
and hold you tight.

Your presence on earth is calming and joyful.

I long to sit with you in a quiet space,
hold your hand, and whisper,
"You are beautiful."

XLV

The scent of your perfume drifts
into my olfactory
and I turn around.

You stand in the doorway
with a sultry lean
and glance in my direction.

As your soul's gravity pulls me in,
I take you into my arms
and hold you tight.

Our hearts beat together,
the world disappears,
and you become my everything.

I live in the eternity of this moment
and hope you feel my love.

XLVI

I am haunted
by the desire of you.

I can feel your presence
and the need to kiss you is overwhelming.

Whisper my name
and command your wish.

Love has bound me to you
and intertwined our essences.

XLVII

It would be fun to explore
love with you:

Holding hands.
Being in your presence.
Knowing you are there.

Let me welcome you home with a kiss
and have your goodness wash over me.

XLVIII

A feeling of contentment
and longing surrounds me
as I picture your face.

Your profound beauty affects me
in a deep way.

I see perfection in your eyes
and eternity in your lips.

I could inhabit your being forever
and be happy there.

XLIX

I do not sing your praises lightly.
You are not a fleeting fancy.

You are magnificent
and worthy of my devotion.

I give you my everything.

I give you my love
and expect nothing in return.

Oh my God...
Who am I kidding?

I want to hold you tightly
and kiss your exquisite lips.
I want your heat.
I want your body to tremble in waves of pleasure.
I want us to meld into one.
I want my name whispered during your exhale.
I want you.

ᒪ

There's a ripple in the universal aether
and I feel your core clutch me.

The strength of your embrace is comforting
and the warmth of your soul is feverish.

Both beautiful and everlasting
your importance is immense.

ել

You transcend beauty
and attraction.

An aura of eminence surrounds
and lifts you.

You are a primal force
and I must follow.

As I submit to your charms,
my head bowed before you,
you raise my chin with your fingers
and gaze into my eyes.

With a movement of your lips,
you speak my name as a blessing.

Your power is eternal and I am yours.

LII

Sometimes,
when it's after the witching hour,
I remember the ecstasy we have experienced:

The feel of your lips,
the touch of your muscular body,
and the moans of your mouth.

You are a Goddess!

LIII

A world of joy lies behind
the veil of your smile.

Let it be my beacon
and guide me to life's happiness.

The light of the world flows through you.

LIV

I miss the primal celebration
of the carnal that we pursued together.

I would love to spend the evening
talking and playing.

I need to worship you again!

LV

Close your eyes
and release yourself.

Float out of your body
and merge with the universal aura.
You will see my essence waiting there.

Drift towards me.

Let us hold each other
and contemplate eternity.

Your energy makes life worthwhile.

LVI

Your beauty is a lightning bolt.

It streaks across the sky
and imprints my cornea.

Although it flashed in an instant,
I close my eyes
and see you radiate before me.

LVII

A thread of passion flows through me
like a river born of a mountain spring.
You are the source.

It bubbles to the surface
and I feel you near me.

An unconquerable spirit
that overwhelms me with loveliness.

LVIII

The fire of your regard falls upon me
and I am exhilarated to be among the chosen.

A world of joy lives in your eyes.

LIX

Your name forms on my lips
as a mystical whisper.

With a rumbling invocation,
I connect to your power,
access the Goddess,
and feel her love.

Your importance is immeasurable
and cannot be denied.

Let me be worthy of your esteem.

LX

Love fills my heart
and your name shapes the letters.

You sit upon a golden throne
and survey your domain.

You are always in my thoughts
and command the happiness of my memories.

To see you again would be a blessing,
but to kiss you
and taste your sweet lips...

That would be heaven!

LXI

You are the beauty
that helps me get through the day.

I imagine your illumination
and everything becomes brighter.

LXII

As your essence licks my lips,
your magick dances with my tongue
and fills my mind.

I close my eyes
and feel your perfumed touch
flow over my skin like smooth velvet.

Whisper your desires.

I am yours
and long for you to be mine.

LXIII

Your light burns bright
and leads the way.

You have climbed a mountain
and accomplished a dream.

The time has come to change the world.

Embrace yourself
and be the way!

LXIV

On the quest of infinite beauty,
I grasp at the sun
and hope for contentment.

LXV

You are beauty's icon.

I miss the tangible importance
of your being
and the magick that radiates
from your soul.

Your embrace is happiness.

Will you reach into the universe
and hold me?

LXVI

I must fall on my knees
in the face of your glory.

Let me lift you up
and show you to the world.

Your radiance is a beacon
to those who are lost.

Break your fetters
and expose your beauty
to the world!

LXVII

There's a hidden world in your smile,
a place of happiness and joy.

I imagine it shining upon me
and my day becomes brighter.

You are fantastic
and the source of my dreams.

May I be anointed
with your grace and soothed.

LXVIII

After reaching through time and space,
a discovery has been made:

The ancients carved marble
that fading gods imbued
with breathing life.

You are the pinnacle of their creation.

Your toned muscles
and perfectly flowing form
imprint on me.

I am in awe of you.

I give you my internal flame
as a sign of devotion.

LXIX

There's a supple fire
burning between us.

The heat smolders
and singes our skin.

I love the pleasure of its pain.

Let us stoke the flame
until we are engulfed.

Our bodies charred
beyond recognition.

Then use your lips
as a salve to heal me.

LXX

Absorb the light
and be the birth of a new dawn.

Your beauty is the core of creation.
You bring inspiration and life.

As the radiation of your being absorbs into my self,
I feel imbued with power and strength.

With you as my partner,
I can conquer the world.

LXXI

A beam of light blasts from the sky
and pins me through my third eye.
The immaterial world floods my brain.

Using a frantic twist,
I attempt to release myself,
but it's to no avail.

I am overwhelmed
by the extrasensory.

Divining my need,
you travel the breeze
and seek me out.

With a flow of beauty,
you wrap me in the strength of your core,
covering me in a force of calm.

My visions focus and I can see the truth:

You are my lodestar and my anchor.
You keep me grounded and on course.

LXXII

You stand before me
in a fashionable rosé wrap
exuding a confident beauty.

Let us remove our layers,
unburden ourselves,
and expose our souls.

Pull the bow of your dress,
and open it to the air.

As you slide the fabric to the floor,
a blush glows over your skin.
You are majestic in your nudity.

My eyes flow over your delicious curves
as my blood rushes through my veins.
I must stop myself from devouring you.

LXXIII

Release the world
and come with me.

We will be a nation unto ourselves
with pleasure as our currency.

I will bankrupt us.

To become solvent,
I must borrow
from the gold standard of your allure,
eternal and everlasting.

LXXIV

Shed your artificial skin
and let me see you
as God intended.

The flow of your flesh inspires awe.

I love the shy grace contained
in the movement of your valleys and hills.

My breath shortens
as you breathe in deep
and walk towards me.

Your arms wrap around me
and the heat of your body joins mine.

With a whispered tickle, your lips murmur.
"Join me in my nakedness.
The time for an offering has arrived."

LXXV

An echo of the clock's ringing
leaves midnight behind
with me alone and awake.

The dream of you dances
on the tip of my tongue
as I silently form your name on my lips.

I taste the residue of recently explored passion.

During daylight,
you are never far from my thoughts.

During the witching hour,
I can feel your spirit intertwined with mine.

Your beauty lifts me
as the burn of your soft touch inspires me.
I drift to sleep holding the idea of you.

LXXVI

On a blanket in a grassy meadow,
we hold hands
while staring into eternity.

A comet streaks
and trails stardust in its wake.

As the particles drift down,
they absorb into our bodies.

We are the infinite.
We define creation.

The spark of life ignites
through our joining.
You become me and I become you.

Together we elevate life...
into the sacred,
into the godhead,
into the boundless cosmic.

LXXVII

As wind licks its way through oak branches,
you use it as your voice to whisper my name.

"Seek me in the East."

I follow your command and begin my journey.
You are the grail I quest for.

"Find me in the West."

After traveling towards the rising sun,
my destination is in sight behind me.

"Enjoy me in the North."

We are each other's reward.
Let us wallow in flesh and discover passion.

"Destroy me in the South."

Leaving is sweet sorrow.
I return home, but will never be the same.
Your imprint is upon my soul.

LXXVIII

A hidden strength bubbles
below your surface.

It is your true power.
Nothing can remove it.

Reach through the clouds
and expose your sun.

Let your light shine
and chase the darkness away.

Remember:
You are love.

LXXIX

When we are dust and bones, fear not!
We shall not be forgotten.

A weary scholar
will burn the midnight oil
and find traces of us
hidden in poems.

The threads of our existence
will be painstakingly pieced together
and woven into a tapestry.

Our eternal fidelity will be held high
as the purest form of love.

Nothing is stronger
than life captured in literature.

LXXX

With the waning light of dawn's resurgence,
we commence the ceremony of making.

Tie me to your altar
and mark me with the sigil of a rope's burn.

My body is yours to ravage.

Bury your face in the hollow of my neck
and taste its flesh with your coarse tongue.

Turn my lips into your sanctuary
and find your peace there.

The mysteries of magick swirl around us.

Our energies mix together
and we are stronger.

LXXXI

Gaze at the moon,
behold the sky.
Love doesn't end
after we die.

It transmutes and expands
to eclipse the earth.
Greater than the heavens
if you calculate its worth.

Give of yourself,
but don't give in.
You don't have to fight
in order to win.

Just release your soul
into her hands,
and rest assured everything
will go according to plan.

Acknowledgments

I would like to thank the people who support me.

Evy Zen for keeping my poetry polished.

Everly Yours Designs for the beautiful cover.

Georgia for reading my manuscript.

Olivia for her friendship and kind words.

My Muse for her inspiration.

About the Author

Andrew Chiniche has lived in Hawaii, the Virgin Islands, and Florida, but his favorite place is in the worlds of books and movies. He believes every work of fiction contains truth hidden in the wonderful and fantastic.

Andrew received a degree in English Literature from Mississippi State University, and currently lives in Alabama.

His first poetry collection, Love's Dawn, was released in 2018.

Moon Image source:
https://www.freeiconspng.com/img/44673

www.ingramcontent.com/pod-product-compliance
Lightning Source LLC
Chambersburg PA
CBHW052015170626
46808CB00007B/2939